COME...
KILL ME AND
COMPLETE
YOUR FINAL
TASK!

Clink
Clop

ECHO!

8

LET'S GO, GROWL.

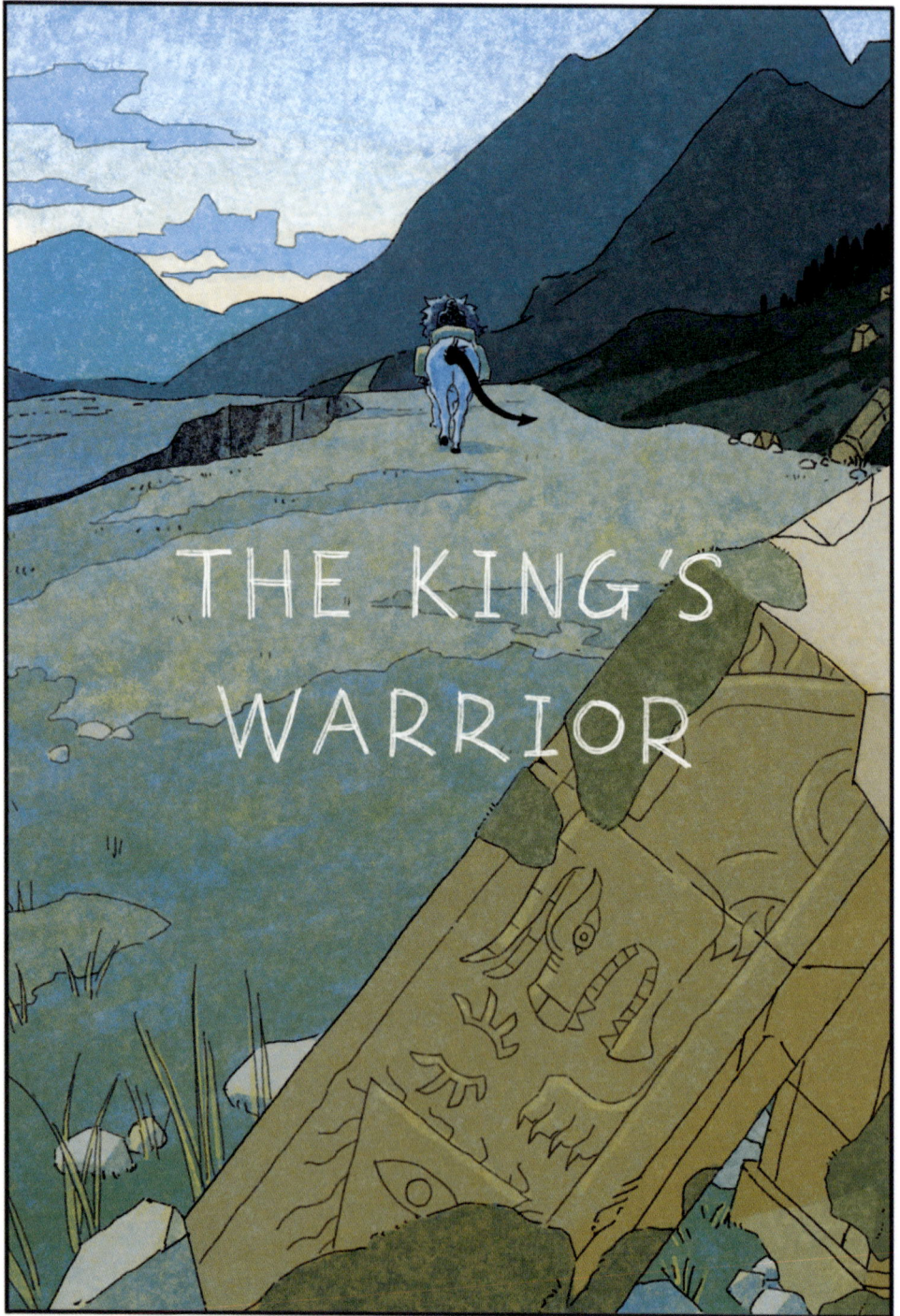

THE KING'S
WARRIOR

TO THE END OF THIS LAND. THERE YOU'LL FIND A BLACK CASTLE.

IN THE CASTLE LIVES AN ALCHEMIST, IMMENSELY POWERFUL AND WICKED. HE IS THE FINAL THREAT TO OUR GOLDEN CITY.

KILL HIM FOR ME.

UPON YOUR RETURN, YOU AND YOUR BROTHER CAN GO AND LIVE AS YOU WISH.

AFTER SO MANY YEARS, YOU TWO WILL HAVE SO MUCH CATCHING UP TO DO.

THIS MAP IS WRONG, GROWL. WE SHOULD BE BEYOND THE KINGDOM'S BORDERS.

HO!

GOOD TO SEE A LIVING PERSON! TRAVELERS HAVE BEEN A RARE SIGHT AROUND HERE.

HELLO, DO YOU KNOW THE WAY TO THE BLACK CASTLE?

HOW MANY LIVES DO YOU HAVE, YOUNG FRIEND? THAT PLACE IS INHABITED BY DEMONS. NO ONE DARES TO GO NEAR.

LISTEN TO ME, FOR YOUR SAFETY IT'S BEST IF YOU...YRRK...

A CHIMERA HERE...?

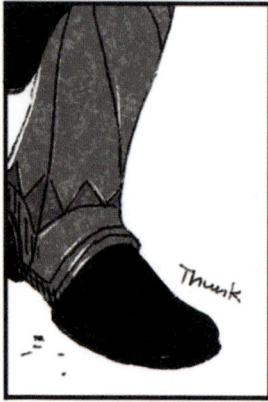

EXCUSE ME, DO YOU KNOW ABOUT THE BLACK CASTLE?

SORRY, I'M IN A HURRY.

IF YOU AREN'T BUYING, JUST LEAVE!

YOUR GRANDPA'S NOT HERE TODAY, KID?

I WOULD SAY, THESE ARE WORTH ONLY HALF THE PRICE.

THESE ARE ALL SEWN WITH SNAKE SCALES OF GOOD QUALITY. I WON'T—

HOW ABOUT YOU GIVE ME A FEW,

AND I'LL TAKE CARE OF THEM FOR YOU—HAH!

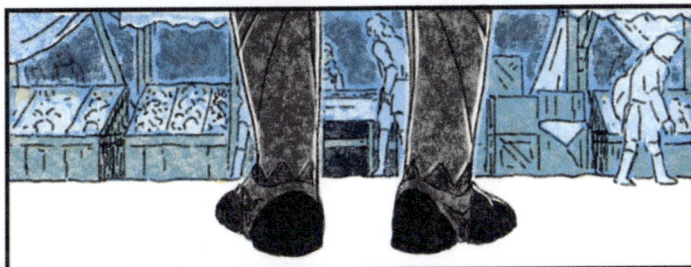

WHAT ARE YOU LOOKING AT!

LEAVE HER BE.

MIND YOUR OWN BUSINESS, OUTSIDER...

A LIONSTEED!

YOU'RE ONE OF THOSE BASTARDS FROM THE GOLDEN CITY...

......WHAT HAPPENED TO YOUR VILLAGE?

THE CAVALRY OF THE GOLDEN CITY INVADED US. THE MEN WERE TAKEN AWAY AND THE VILLAGE WAS LOOTED.

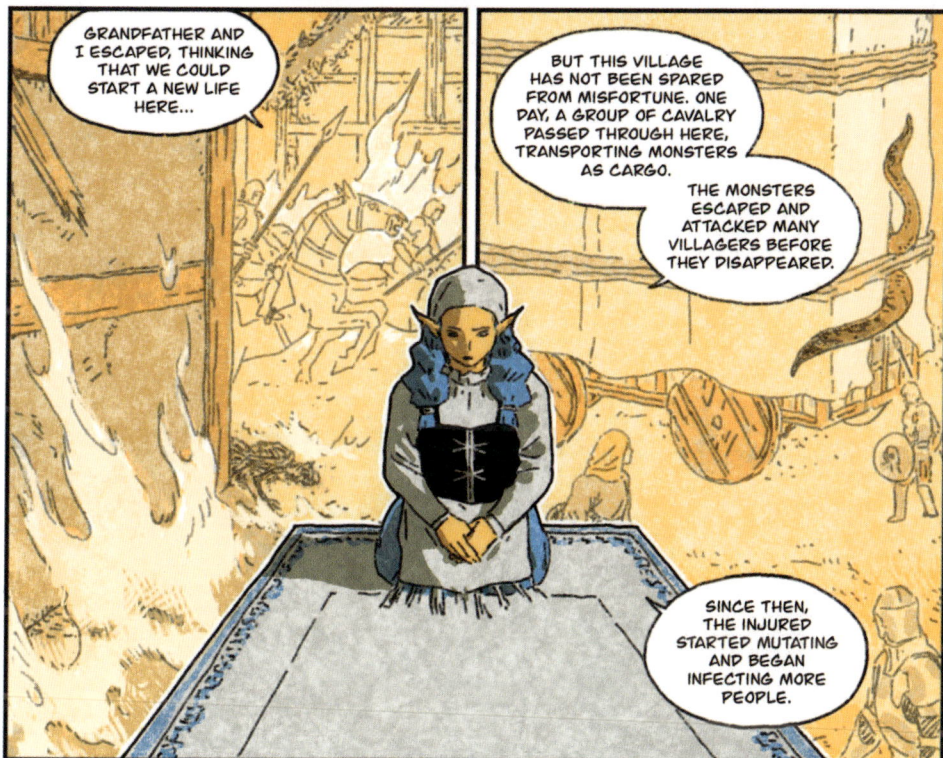

GRANDFATHER AND I ESCAPED, THINKING THAT WE COULD START A NEW LIFE HERE...

BUT THIS VILLAGE HAS NOT BEEN SPARED FROM MISFORTUNE. ONE DAY, A GROUP OF CAVALRY PASSED THROUGH HERE, TRANSPORTING MONSTERS AS CARGO.

THE MONSTERS ESCAPED AND ATTACKED MANY VILLAGERS BEFORE THEY DISAPPEARED.

SINCE THEN, THE INJURED STARTED MUTATING AND BEGAN INFECTING MORE PEOPLE.

I ASK YOU NOT TO SEEK THE BLACK CASTLE. I HEARD THAT DEMONS RESIDE THERE, TURNING SIMPLE BEASTS INTO MONSTERS.

THEY SAY THAT THE MONSTERS ARE TERRIFYING, COVERED WITH STRANGE LIMBS. THEY ARE MINIONS OF DEMONS.

IF YOU INSIST ON GOING, THE BRIDGE TO THE CASTLE IS SOUTHEAST OF HERE.

I'LL PRAY FOR YOU AND GRANDFATHER.

WHERE IS YOUR GRANDFATHER?

HE'S ONE OF THE FEW WHO HASN'T BEEN INFECTED. HE WENT TO THE TOWN TO SELL GOODS THIS MORNING.

......

HE SHOULD BE BACK IN TWO OR THREE DAYS.

I HOPE HE COMES BACK SAFELY.

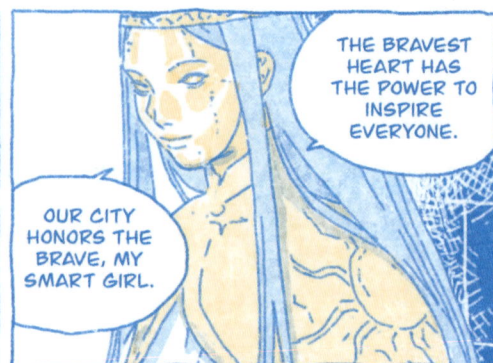

A LIONSTEED...

AAAAH!

THE CAVALRY FROM THE GOLDEN CITY ARE ATTACKING!!

MARA, MY FIERCEST WARRIOR,

WELL DONE.

LONG LIVE THE KING OF GOLD!

HOW BEST TO REWARD THE ONE I TRUST ABOVE ALL OTHERS...?

MAYBE JUST...

SET US FR—

I'LL TAKE OVER THE WATCH. THERE'S STILL SOME TIME BEFORE DAWN.

I'M OKAY, GROWL.

SO MANY...

WE MOVE SWIFTLY, GROWL.

THERE'S NO WAY SHE HOLDS IT OFF FOR SO LONG...

SHE'S JUST A LITTLE GIRL.

ECHO, HANG IN THERE...

I'LL KILL THIS THING RIGHT AWAY!

WHAT
TH...

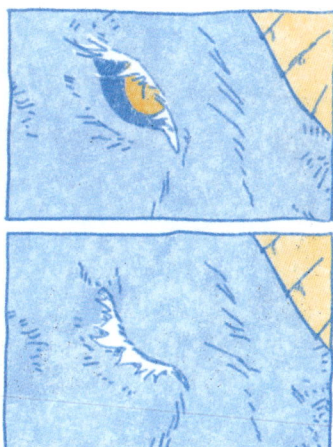

WAIT FOR
ME ECHO,
JUST A LITTLE
LONGER.

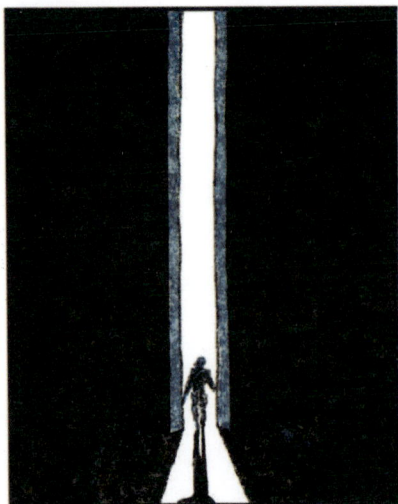

HEEHEE...
HEE...

HEE...
HEE...

I WAS WORRIED YOU WOULD DIE ON YOUR JOURNEY.

YOU'RE... THE ALCHEMIST...

SURELY YOU HAVE MORE QUESTIONS THAN THAT.

OH, TAKE A SEAT. THE WINE IS READY.

THE KING SENT YOU TO SLAY ME. BUT YOU SEE, YOU DON'T NEED TO LIFT A FINGER.

I'M TOO OLD TO MOVE ANYWAY. GIVEN A FEW DAYS, I'LL BE GONE.

WHAT DO YOU MEAN?

THE KING EXILED YOU.

I GUESS YOUR MOUNT IS DEAD? YOU CAN'T GO BACK ANYMORE.

YEARS AGO I CAME TO THIS CASTLE ON THE KING'S COMMAND. AFTER ALL MY YEARS CREATING CHIMERAS, HIS HIGHNESS TASKED ME WITH MAKING AN ULTIMATE CHIMERA ARMY.

SOON I DISCOVERED NOTHING BUT ROT IN THIS DESOLATE PLACE... AND ON THE OTHER SIDE OF THE BRIDGE, GUESS WHAT I FOUND?

ALL MY FAILED CHIMERAS, EACH ONE SO FAMILIAR, NOW KEEPING ME TRAPPED HERE. HOW RUTHLESS MY KING IS!

61